CAN WE CALL IT A DESTINY

PRITAM SINGH

शक़्रिया इस सोशल मीडिया वाली दुनिया को छोड़ कर,

मेरी कागज पर लिखे दुनिया में आने के लिए.

Thank you for leaving this Social Media world and coming to my paper world.

Contents

Acknowledgements

This book isn't just a book; it's the beginning of my writing career.
Writing this book wasn't easy for me.
I have given my sleepless nights and hardworking days to this book, and it would not have been possible to write it without the blessings, love, and infinite support of you.
Mummy, Papa, and Bhaiya.
Thank you Ganpatti Bappa for always showering your blessing on me.

ONE

THE FAILED BOOK LAUNCH

The LOL CAFÉ: A place where the unknown becomes known, and the known becomes unknown. A place where many hearts were broken, and many hearts began to beat on the repeat. A place where a love story expires without the expiration date being known.

Hello, this is Tarini Talwar, owner of "THE LOL CAFE" and the narrator of this story.

My story started on a cold, rainy day when I was sitting alone in the corner area of my café, drinking a cup of coffee, and watching people running here and there, covering their heads with their hands. Some eventually found shelter, while some strangers tried to make friends by sharing their umbrellas.

"Hey, hello! Is anyone there?" A soft voice came from the reception counter. I quickly took a sip of coffee and walked to the reception area.

As a table moved in front of my eyes, I saw an almost 5.7 feet long light-skinned boy wearing black cargo pants and a white shirt with a black sweater, along with white transparent glasses and matte black shoes. His short hair and goatee beard made his personality appear more mature than his actual age.

"Hello, sir. What would you like to have?" I asked as soon as I put on my apron and walked to the other side of the reception.

"You............." he tried to guess.

"What?" I gave him the reaction.

"You are Tarini Talwar, right?"

He asked and eyed the empty café, moving his head slightly.

"Unfortunately, yes!" I replied with a smile.

"Hi, I am Arjuna Bhatt." He extended his hand to me,

I reciprocated and we both shook hands.

"Tell me, what would you like to have?" I asked again.

"Your café!" He answered.

"Excuse me?" I quickly reacted.

"No! I mean, I am a debutante writer and I want to promote my book here today. It will only take half an hour" he explained clearly.

"But there's no one else in the café today except for me," I said.

"Yes, I can see that. How about tomorrow?" He asked gently.

"Umm.....okay, that sounds good, but you'll have to pay for it," I said.

"Pay..........?" He thinks a little.

"Okay, but how much?" He asked a moment later.

"?200 per hour only," I answered.

"Okay, done! I'll see you tomorrow," he said.

"Okay, see you then," I said.

"Bye!" He said and walked away happily.

After that, I put on a few old songs on a loop and returned to the same corner area I was in before.

A Day Later

It was 11:10 A.M. and in the capacity of 40-50 seats, only 12 seats were occupied by the customers inside the café.

"Knock-knock!" a sound entered my ears from the main door. As I took a few steps towards the main door, I saw Arjuna trying to open the main door while holding two medium-sized boxes that almost covered his face. I walked up to him and pushed the main door open as a gesture of help.

"Thank you!" He said as he embarks into the café.

"Do you need any help with these boxes?" I asked.

"No-No, I'm good," he said. However, struggling with the boxes.

"So, what's in it?" I asked, pointing through the boxes.

"Books! No, I mean my own signed copies," He said.

"Oh! okay, but you know what? I think I should help you, it looks heavier," I said.

"No, thanks, books never feel heavier to me." He said with an immediate smile on his face.

"Okay, then do your thing! Good luck," I wished him.

"Yeah, thank you!" he said. He after walks into the middle of the café and put the boxes on the table. he got all his books out on another table and aesthetically decorated the table.

I was at the reception counter, glimpsing at him as he made a pyramid with his books on the table. Some people were looking at him curiously, while some of them were ignoring him. After decorating the table he went to all those 12 seats which were occupied by the customers and requested them to move their chairs towards him and pay attention to him, for a few minutes some of them gave himattention, but some didn't. As he incites discussing his book, almost everybody shifted their chair back in place and pretended to be busy with their stuff.

Arjuna's confidence and enthusiasm was shattered, and his body language gets low, He breaks down the pyramid and settles all the books into the boxes again.

"Hi," he uttered as he reached the reception counter.

"What! You are done?" I asked.

"Unfortunately yes, but forgot that, and tell me how much I will have to pay you?"

"*You don't have to!*"

Why?

"*Because you just took 15 minutes and these folks didn't appreciate your talent either.*"

"*So, sorry, I can't take the money,*" *I said while pointing toward the people inside the café.*

"*How do you know, I am talented?*"

"*Writing a book isn't easy, so I guess you are talented,*" *I said.*

"*So you are a bookworm?*"

Yes, I lied.

"*Can I get some coffee and cookies, please?*" *A new customer asked as he appeared at the reception counter.*

"*Yes, please wait at table number 15 there,*" *I said, indicating the table.*

"Sure," the customer departed to the table. I gawked at Arjuna's eyes, it was fully red as if he wanted to cry over his failure.

"Listen, this is for you," said Arjuna, as he lay over a copy of his book on the reception counter.

"Thank you & Bye!" He said, and left in a hurry Although I wanted to talk to him, I wanted to know him, but after noticing his low body language and his sentimental face, I couldn't muster up the courage to ask for his phone number.

As he withdrew, I made a cup of coffee and served it at table number 15.

TWO
PARENT'S CALL

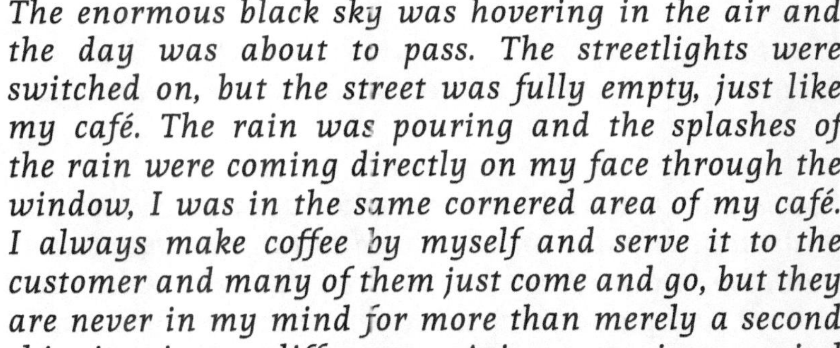

The enormous black sky was hovering in the air and the day was about to pass. The streetlights were switched on, but the street was fully empty, just like my café. The rain was pouring and the splashes of the rain were coming directly on my face through the window, I was in the same cornered area of my café. I always make coffee by myself and serve it to the customer and many of them just come and go, but they are never in my mind for more than merely a second this time it was different as Arjuna was in my mind since the morning, His face was coming into my mind over and over. My inner soul wanted him to come, sit next to me and talk to me, but why all these were happening? I didn't know, I was confused, and so I started pondering. Abruptly, my phone ranged.

"Hello, papa!" I said.

"Hi Beta, so how is it going?" Asked my papa.

"*Everything is fine, but why are you asking?*"

Listen, "your grandmother is not well, and she wanted all of us to be with her for some days in the village."

"*But what happened to her, is she Alright?*" *I inquired.*

"*Yes, she is, but not exactly.*"

"*Doctors are assuming that it might be her last Monsoon this year.*" *Explained my Dad emotionally.*

"*Look, dad, you and mom have just got retired and you guys have enough time to spend with grandma, but as you also know, I have just started the café and I can't close it easily and come with you, that too, for a week.*"

"*Tarini, your grandmother loves you.*"

"*I know, dad, but please try to understand.*" *I requested dad, but until then, my mom had already borrowed the phone from my father's hand.*

"*No! We are not going to understand you this time, you have to come.*" *Ordered my mom.*

"But mom, what about my café?" I asked.

"It's just a café Tarini, People will not sleep hungry if you close your café for a week," my mom shouted and continued;

"Is the café now become bigger than your grandmother's health?"

"No way, mom!" I lied.

"Then take the first flight and come. we will be in the village.

"I know that you don't hate her, and I also know that you don't like to be out of your comfort zone, but this time you will have to come."

"Doctors are also assuming that..........."

"I know! Dad, just tell." I intrupted

"Then just come, Tarini."

She said and disconnected the call emotionally.

Love is the only thing that I never understood properly. I guess when you like to be with someone whom you can hug anytime, whom you miss every second when they're not near, and whom you can talk to endlessly is what love is, but I didn't feel any of these emotions for my grandmother.

For me, she was just an old woman whom I gave respect, that's it. But now, just because of her, I'll have to close my café.

Well, what can I do rather than obey my parents?

So I eventually went inside my room, crossing through the reception area. I put on my blue denim jeans and a white hoodie, paired with my transparent glasses and black and white shoes. I pack my bag and walk towards the reception counter to get the keys. As I opened the drawer, I saw the keys were beside Arjuna's book. I grabbed the keys along with his book, but didn't know why I picked his book; I don't know. Maybe because of his unique book cover, I don't know why, but my mind compelled me to pick his book. I locked my home cum café and left downstairs to take the cab or something till then the weather had become nicer.

The rain has been stopped and the empty street which was till now filled with water started filling with some people going in and out. I flung my bag onto my shoulder, but Arjuna's book was still in my hand, and I didn't know why I didn't keep the book inside the bag. The train station wasn't that far, so I started walking.

"Hey, "The LoL café" right?" I heard from my back, and as I turned, I saw a bright girl on a yellow-colored scooter. A little shorter than me, wearing a black cap, on red blonde hair.

"Yes! Do I know you?" I asked, approaching her.

"No, you don't know me, but I know you."

"But how?"

"Hi, I am Dhara. I have been to your café many times."

"Oh....... Okay, sorry, I am very bad with faces and names," I said and we shook hands.

"So you are going somewhere?" She asked as she stared at my bag.

"Yes, just the nearby train station," I said.

"Bro...who takes the train these days?" She questioned.

"I guess those who can not afford plane tickets," I answered back in sarcasm, and we both laughed.

"Okay, then come, I will drop you at the station."

"No, I will manage, don't worry."

"I know you will manage by yourself, but come, I will drop you off. I am going there only." She insisted. Suddenly her phone beeped as she notices the message, I take a view of the street, the side lamps were flickering and as the evening was passing by the empty street was getting darker. As soon as she skims her massage, I settled myself in the back seat of her scooter and become her companion for a few minutes.

"Comfortable?" She asked and began riding.

"Yes, By the way, what do you do Dhara?" I asked her just for the small talk.

"I think you didn't notice my T-shirts, I am a delivery girl. I deliver food at night." She said.

Oh! Okay.

"But, where we're you heading right now?" I asked.

"Just near the station to deliver Some Pizzas."

"Oh! Okay, who eats pizza after so much heavy rain?" I whispered, putting Arjuna's book inside the bag.

"There are some hungry frogs," She responded, and we both started laughing.

THREE

READING VIA TRAGEDY

A few moments later, she dropped me off outside the railway station and sped away, as she was getting late for her delivery order. I entered the railway station and was immediately assaulted by the loud, annoying sound of the train engine. The station was filled with a plethora of people, from whom I had only one question: where do they go every day? I wasn't able to adjust to the noise and the crowds, but somehow I managed. Suddenly I saw a train slowly pacing from platform no. 2 and wondered where it was going. So, I asked an uncle, and he replied that "it was the only train heading to Bihar today." As soon as I heard this news, I pushed a few people and started running like Geet of "Jab We Met" to catch the train, but there was no Bhaisaheb giving me hands from the door of the train.

I ran from platform 1 to 2, grabbed the door handle of the train, and jumped inside.

My legs started shivering, my heartbeat started beating, my breath became heavier, and my throat became dry.

However, I was happy with my running performance and also because I had finally boarded the train. I was happy for a moment, but then I saw a T.T dressed in black checking a woman's ticket. I remembered that I had forgotten to take my own ticket, and now the T.T could drag me out off the train or fine me heavily at any time. I looked around, and there was no empty seat for me, so I sat on the floor near the door and took out my water bottle from my bag. I made my parched throat a water park.

As I fill my parched tummy, I feel that my phone was not in my pocket, so I stood up while checking my pants, but it was not there. Astonishingly, I search my bag, but the phone was not there too. In my vein and my brain, every organ in my body was only worrying about the phone. My wilful mind was not willing to accept this tragedy.

But who can alter the happenings?

My intuition was telling me that I might have slipped it down while catching the train.

Who knows, what happened to it? Maybe someone found it, or maybe it got run over by the train. I was so angry, I punched the train door. Then, after 15 minutes of just thinking about my lost phone, I decided to eat the cookies I always carry with me when I travel.

Amid taking out the cookies from the bag, my attention was drawn to Arjuna's book. I took out his book and gaze at the content of the book, there were only six chapters with merely 175 pages in his book.

Although, even reading six chapters is no less than climbing a mountain for me. I remember the last time I read a novel I was in class seven, but the train journey will also not be going to be a cakewalk for me as it was not a trip of some 2 hours journey. It will take 18 to roughly 20 hours to reach my village in Bihar and that too without the phone, I had nothing else to do rather than just sit on the train floor so, I thought why not just read Arjuna's book.

FOUR

THE VILLAGE TRIP

19 Hours Later

This was the first time I was travelling without the tickets hiding from the T.T and also reading a novel. It was a new and exciting experience, and I was fascinated by the world around me. If now my old friends had seen me like this, they would have gone insane. However, I also become insane after reading Arjuna's book, I didn't realize when I finished five chapters of his book. His story of love flowed like a poem and touched my heart. He narrated the story in his extraordinary style, I don't know why people were not buying his book, but I was happy that he gifted me the book.

I, this time, desperately initiated to read the last chapter of his book, but suddenly an irksome sound came into my ears. It was the same train engine sound as I peek outside the train, I notice a banner written "Welcome to Bihar" on it. The train halts with a jerk, I instantly put the book inside the bag and get off the train. People

were hurrying to go to their respective places.

Some people were eating samosas at the nearby thela wherein some were waiting for the next train to attain. There was so much hustle and bustle. Somehow I made my space and come out of the train station. Many black and yellow colored autos were parked across the road. The drivers were shouting the name of the locations where they usually go. As one of the drivers shouted my village's name, I traverse the road and went to him shortly.

"Please sit, madam!" said the driver as he spat up the gutka from his mouth.

"But what about the money?" I asked.

"Only 50 rupees, madam," he replied.

"No! What about 35?" I said.

"40 is final, madam!" He said.

"Okay, let's go then," I said, relaxing inside the auto. The driver plugin some old songs and started the auto. I took out Arjuna's book from my bag and started reading the last chapter.

"You are here to give some kind of exam, madam?"

The auto wala inquired casually.

"No! Why?"

"No, you are reading a book, so I thought....."

"Oh... no, it's a novel, not an educational book."

"Yeah, whatever!" he said, and speed up the auto. I get back into reading and after 12 minutes the auto entered the aisles of my village. It was fully changed, the houses were now made up of bricks and cement. Women were preparing food on the gases and cylinders. The roads were now much better than before and all the houses have their dish connections. The farmers were farming with modern types of equipment and much more, it seems like the village had become modern. Looking at all these changes, I think they had

chosen a really good government "kyuki acche din toh such mein aagaye hai." The auto stopped at the main entrance of my home as I told him (Autowala) to stop. I paid him his 40 rupees and leg it out of his auto. I observe people were staring at me as if trying to guess who am I.

The auto veered around and left, I knock on the main heavy wooden door of my home but nobody responded. I once again knock on the door, much harder than before. As the main door opened, and I went inside, I saw my father wearing white pants and a shawl with a monkey cap his fair complexion and medium height were giving me a resemblance to some cartoon character.

"Hey, what happened, why were you not answering our calls?

We were trying to call you since the last we talked, You know your mom got so worried." conveyed my father from a distance.

"And you, you were not worried, Papa?" I raised a question.

"You........(He take a pause)" Yes I too was worried," my father said and we both hugged.

"Nothing had happened, dad, it was just that my phone dropped at the train station," I said as we both began walking from my garden toward our living room.

"But who told you to take the train, why don't you come via plane?" He asked a little annoyingly. I restrain silent and just walks in behind him, he turned and stares at me.

"Beta I know you are a self-independent girl, and you can manage everything on your own, but God had made families so that they can share good times as well as bad times, why do you never ask your parents for money?"

"It's not about the money, papa, I just wanted a train trip, now please end this money topic here."

"Okay, then let's go to your grandmother's room," he said, and we both attain grandmother. The room was fully atheistic, an old fan was moving slowly, the bed was in the center of the room and grandma was resting on it. She was covered with several blankets, I could only see her white hair and her dark brown face.

"Namaste Dadi, (Hello grandmother)" I said while touching her feet for blessings.

"Hey, my daughter, when did you come? Look how skinny you have become.

Don't you eat some food though, you have your own shop?" said my grandmother as she holds my hand.

I sit beside her on the bed, her bedroom was smelling somewhat like a public hospital.

The smell of medicine was the theme of the bedroom.

So "how are you Tarini, how's everything?" My Grandmother asked in her extremely sluggish and metered voice.

"Fine dadi! But how are you feeling now?"

"Extremely happy!"

"I thought you wouldn't come, but you are here finally."

"Arey, I am always one call away dadi," as I mumbled this, my dad and grandmother began to laugh.

Unexpectedly, a woman enters the room. Looking at my dad and grandmother's joyful laugh, she also starts laughing.

"Tarini go tell your mom that Simar Ji is here," said my dad while controlling his laugh. I step out of the room, guessing why they began laughing. The sound of the chorus was coming out directly from the kitchen which was located close to my grandmother's room, as I entered the kitchen room I saw mom was cleaning some kitchen utensils I went close to her without making any sound and hugged her from her back.

"What are you doing, Ravish? Your mother is in the next room and simar Ji too could come anytime." She assumed me to be her husband, my father, who was hugging her.

"Maa, it's me!" She whirls back, her eyes left hefty, and she refuses to do eye contact.

"Oh, it's you! I thought........" she stops saying.

"Sorry, what did you think?" I teased her with a smirking smile.

"When did you arrive?" She inquired while hugging me tightly.

"Just now!" I said.

"And why were you not answering our calls? We got so scared."

"It's a long story maa, I will tell you later, but now some simar Ji had come to Grandma's room."

"Oh, she came, she is the nurse of your grandmother," mom said.

"Oh, but why is she here in the morning?" I asked.

"She comes every day to vaccinate your grandmother." my mom explained.

"And why is she taking injections?" I asked.

"High Diabetes!" she asserted and left. I grab a water bottle from the fridge and went straight to my room. It was completely clean, some of my old hand paintings were on the wall opposite the bed. The room was fully changed, but the vibe of the room was still the same. I toss my bag and the bottle onto the bed and opened the window instantly.

The morning pristine fresh air absorbs in my heart and my entire body. The view from the window was stunning, I can see mountains, clouds, fog, and many green grounds which were filled with wheat crops.

After a while, I went inside my washroom and had a good childlike water bath, and then stumbled on my bed and nodded off.

FIVE

MAILING LOVE BEGAN

5 Hours Later

The sun was on our heads and the winds were absorbing our breaths, the wheat crops were hugging each other, while the bright blue skies were dancing with the air. The windows of my room had been open for the last 5 hours as the heavy afternoon wind strike on my eyes, I woke up yawning from my mouth. The village was so silent in the afternoon that for a second I thought I had become deaf, but then cow's moo broke my delusion. I get off my bed and walked down by taking the stairs. Dadi's room was adjacent to the kitchen, so I peeked into her room, the fan was still moving wherein dadi was snoozing on her bed. I went inside the kitchen, mom had prepared "karele ki sabzi, daal and rice" for lunch, although I used to love karela in my childhood as of now I was not able to vibe with its bitter taste. So, I started searching for other things in the kitchen that I can eat.

After a few moments, I found some packets of Maggie on the upper racks. It took me roughly 10 minutes to cook Maggie, although maggie admitted it to be prepared in just 2 minutes. I noticed from the kitchen window that the street was fully empty and not even a single man or woman was wandering on the street. I then fetch my maggie bowl and a bottle of water in both my hands and pace into my parents' bedroom, both of them were sleeping. I step up to my room by taking the stairs and plop the water bottle and the bowl on my bed.

I take out Arjuna's book from the bag to flip through it, although only 12 pages remained to skim, still I eagerly wanted to finish the book ASAP. So, I grab the bowl and the book and crouched at the window, and started reading while eating simultaneously. In an hour I wrapped up reading the whole book and become Arjuna's forever Fan. For me, True love is eternal, infinite, and always like itself, and that is what he had also solidified In his book.

The love story was so greatly rejuvenated with emotion and deep affection that I started sobbing. For a moment I was solely bestowing my heart and soul to the characters of the story and was feeling about the love only. I was not expecting that he could write this kind of love story, but I think that's why it is said that "Don't judge a book by its cover". I wanted to express my feelings, I wanted to call or message him to tell him that he is the most talented author whose book I have ever read, but my awful luck was that I dropped my phone, and now I was not going to buy it from this boring village where most of the people use Zen phone, slice or don't know what type brands of phone.

As I got off from the window, my eyes led way to the back side of the book, where I found Arjuna's Email ID. So, I slowly ran down and entered my parents' room without making any sound and tugged my mother's phone, and went back to my bedroom again. The only intention of taking her phone was that I wanted to mail arjuna and say that he had written a gem, and he should continue doing it So, I opened the e-mail of my mother it was totally weird as she had uploaded a picture of a flying butterfly on her profile and had written her name as "Princess50". I began chuckling at my own after noticing my mom's peculiar though cute childlessness. Her mailbox was filled with various types of clothing offers but avoiding that I wrote an extremely delighted appreciation e-mail and send it to Arjuna. I wasn't expecting a reply from him that quickly but within a minute he mailed back saying "Thank you princess50 glad that you appreciate it and yes I am writing my second book soon."

"I will be the first one to buy your second book as well," I mailed.

"No, you will not be the first one,

I guess you will be the only one," he mailed back.

"No! Why are you saying like that?

There are people who would love to read your book, you just need to promote it well,"

I mailed.

"Well, I did that as well, recently I went to "The LoL Café" in Delhi to promote my book, although the response wasn't good but Tarini the owner of the café was very kind to me as she didn't charge me for promoting my book in her café. She was cute too" he mailed back.

My heart begins bumping, my eyes started blinking, my lips widespread, and my facial color changes to red as if I were a red apple from Kashmir. He was talking about me without even knowing that he was talking to me. So I feel like teasing him a little and knowing what he thinks about me.

"By the way, I have been there a couple of times, but I didn't find her cute at all," I mailed smirking.

"No, she is very cute in my visions. The way she smiles, she talks or the innocence on her face, everything is perfect. The last time when I went there

I wanted to talk to her, but then a customer intrigued and I abandoned." He mailed back.

After glancing at his complimenting e-mail, the very first thing I did was, I jumped onto my bed and started glowing.

Why that customer came at that point in time? I regretted and was about to reply to the mail, but his mail arrived.

"Okay bye, we will chat later and yes if you are coming tonight to the lol café by any chance then please meet me personally. Today I am going there to meet Tarini and also to obtain a co-working space there if she allowed, and yes again TYSM for reading my book.

bye," he mailed.

I mailed him back with a bye emoji.

*The café was closed, yet he will be coming to meet me at the café, but he will not be able to meet me as I am stuck in this fu*king boring village.*

"What an awful fate, god!" I mumbled, but then I interpreted that Arjuna likes me and that is the most important thing. So I stood up on the bed and started dancing.

"What are you doing tarini, have you gone mad?" asserted my mom as she enters the room. I stopped dancing and get off the bed.

"No maa, I have nothing to do here, so I started dancing," I said.

"You have a lot of things to do, go talk to your grandmother." mom suggested.

"But talk about what, mom?" I asked.

"Nothing, just go and sit with her, she will start talking about

something herself," mom said.

Okay, I said and handed over her phone and fled quickly.

4 Hours Later

The day was shifting slowly, Somehow the bright sky had now come to be darker. The street lights were switched on, and some people were walking here and there. I wanted to go outside my home to discover the life of the villagers, but don't know why dadi forcefully stop me and advised me not to go anywhere outside. I obtain her advice positively and started roaming on my terrace. Gradually time passed away, and now the moon was more clear than before.

I took the stairs and came back down to borrow my mother's phone as I was not enjoying being alone on the roof, so I thought of watching something. As I stepped down I saw mom cutting something for dinner whereas dad was discussing something with dadi. It was 7:45 P.M. I grab her (Mom) phone from the dinner table and again stair up to the rooftop. After browsing for a while, finally, my hand stops at a web series called "Brutal murder mystery"

I began watching it and suddenly shut my eyes as it started with a brutal killing of an old woman. As I opened my eyes, Arjuna's mail beeped, I open his e-mail where he had written: "Hi princess50 I hope you didn't go to the lol café, I went there anhour ago the café was closed. So I thought I should inform you."

"Yes I couldn't make it there today, but I am glad that you informed me, thank you," I mailed back.

"It's alright, bye." he mailed.

Initially looking at his e-mail I assumed that it was going to be a long chit-chat but then after seeing his short mail replies which were indicating that he was not interested in having a conversation.

So, I hold him back by mailing:

"Hey by the way I told you she is not cute and now look she is being rude too."

"Who are you talking about?" He mailed back.

"About Tarini, look you went there to meet her, and she closed the café, I mean how rude is that." I mailed back and made an effort to know his feelings about me.

"Hey no! I didn't tell her that I was going to be there and trust me she wasn't rude at all. I think you have somehow misjudged her." He mailed.

"No, I haven't misjudged her. Have you noticed her face properly? Always looks so dull." I mailed back.

"Look, I think she has the most beautiful face in the whole world. Her lips, her eyes, her eyebrows, her cheeks, her hair. The way she talks, the way she smiles, everything looks so, so, so........ extraordinary. Some people would always say dull and all things to others, but they didn't have the guts to put their picture." He mailed in resentment, but the resentment was not for me, it was for @princess50 who was constantly been slamming on Tarini's looks. Although it was me only whom he banged on but after reading his mail, and knowing his protectiveness for tarini I was above the sky.

"Hey, Don't you think it's rude?" I mailed.

"Yeah, sorry! But you shouldn't talk rubbish about her like that." He mailed.

"Oh! So now you are going to protect her from me. Remember, I am the only reader you have." I mailed him with several smiley emojis.

"OO... yes, that's totally gone out of my mind." He mailed with some laughing emojis.

"Hey, I haven't got to know about you anything till now, so tell me what you do?" He asked mailing.

The hardest part is when someone asks you a question, and you have to lie about it but also answer instantly. So my senses proceeded to search for an occupation not as Tarini but as princess50 and unexpectedly my eyes went to a cow that was tied with a rope outside my neighbor's house.

"I have a milk farm and I sell milk." I mailed.

"Milk! Well, I would like to drink your milk," he mailed.

"What?" I mailed as I skim his mail.

"No, sorry, I mistyped.

I mean, I would love to drink your farm's milk," he mailed.

"I hope you would not make these blunders in your second book,"

I mailed him with a few smiling emojis.

"You don't worry, it's in safe hands." he mailed.

"I know, I was just teasing you,

by the way, are you going to meet her again?" I asked mailing.

"Ummm.... Yes, next morning, what about you?" he too asked mailing.

"No, I am a little allergic to cute girls, especially from thosewhose name starts with alphabet T" I mailed with some teasing emojis.

"Shut up! You......." he mailed with Several angry emojis.

"Okay, goodnight Mr. Writer," I mailed him and got off to my parent's room. The room was fully messed up, many of my childhood toys were thrown on the floor and a bundle of papers was on the bed. As I entered the room I saw my father on the bed peering patiently into

those bundles of papers wherein my mom was cleaning some shelves in the room.

"Hey, hello, what you guys are doing?" I asked.

"Nothing beta, we are looking for some property papers," said my dad.

"Oo… okay, Maa here is your phone," I said and put her phone on the bed beside papa and left.

Next afternoon

"Hello! Mr. Writer, what's going on, have you met her today or not?" I mailed him while sitting in the same window of my bedroom. The rain was slowly sprinkling, but the sun was also blazing.

"No, her café was closed today as well. I inquire some people around there, but they said they have no idea," he mailed.

Aww.....how cute, he is going to my café every day just to meet me, I whispered to myself.

"Okay, so what about tomorrow?"

"Yep, I am going tomorrow as well," he mailed back.

I paused for a minute and started assuming if he's serious about me. Because my internal soul would be very happy if he were being serious.

To discover that I mailed him back.

"Hey, why are you going there every day? There are many others co-working spaces," I mailed him in nervousness and started to bite on my nails while guessing, what if he only wants the co-working space and not anything else?

"I know there are many, but I go there just for Tarini" he mailed back.

In quick excitement, I threw my hand in the open air, but it banged into the wall and I broke my nail's extension. I didn't even notice my pain because there was more happiness than a minor pain. Love is blissful when it's a two-way street. A one-sided affair can be painful. So to confirm that I mailed him: "Hey, are you getting in love with her?"

"No!" He mailed immediately. My heartbeat stops beating for a second, my eyes stop blinking my veins stop flowing, and the wind stops blowing in front of me. All of a sudden everything seemed calm but heavy.

His quick reply "No" left me in so much of blankness that I turned pale in a second, but within a second he mailed back where he had written: "No, I mean to say I'm not getting in love with her, I am in love with her since the very first day when I saw her sitting in the corner of the LOL café. I went blown, my mind wasn't in my control, my heartbeat again started beating, and everything started feeling like love" after reading his e-mail, I got down from the window and started dancing heartily in almost every corner of my room. My wide smile was getting wider, my cheeks were now getting pink, my hair started dancing with me in the sink, and my heart was palpitating.

"Are you serious?" I mailed him as I stop enjoying the moment and become princess50@gmail.com.

"100% serious, I am just waiting to meet her, you know I will make effort so that she could also fall for me."

Aww.........how romantic he is, but he doesn't know I am already in love with him. I whispered in my own.

"But how, What type of efforts?" I asked mailing.

"I can't tell you."

"Don't be shy, I didn't ask about your first night," I said.

"Shut up, those things will be between us only," he mailed.

"Us means couple, huh?" I mailed. Annoyingly he sent a "bye emoji" and went offline, I smirk a little.

"Is he kind of shy boy? Whatever, he loves me and that's the best part," I whispered.

SIX

THE END OF VILLAGE TOUR

"Tarini, tarini..........." I gave attention to my mother's intense voice from the kitchen.

I took her phone & went outside of my room asserting "yes maa."

I peeked into my grandma's room, She was as always resting on her bed.

Dad was there too on the wooden chair.

"Why are you looking from there, tarini? Come inside" said my mom as she enters the room holding a bottle of oil from the kitchen.

I shook my head and went inside from her back. My father gives me a sideways glance, he seems to be a little involved in browsing something on Google.My mother sat on the bed with oil beside my grandma and started massaging her legs.

As soon as my grandmother saw me, she gestures me to sit near her. I hold her hand and settle beside her.

"Mom, you were calling me?"

"Yes, your grandmother wants to talk to you," said my mother.

I turned to grandma. "Tarini, you came here to meet me I love that and appreciate that, but I also know that you have just opened your café and closing it for a long period would not be a good idea. It will surely impact your cafe's impression on your regular customer." Explained my grandmother.

"Grandma, I can close that café forever for you," I said, giving a sideways hug to her.

"I know bachha, but still, you should go and focus on your café, I am not going to die any soon. But tarini before going anywhere promise me that you will call me every day."

"I will call you every day Dadi and I can also stay here in the village with you for the rest of my life." As I said, everyone in the room busted out, including dadi-ma.

"What happened, why you guys are laughing?" I asked amidst their laughs. Then I inferred that they might all be laughing at my lies.

"Here's your train ticket Tarini," papa handed over a train ticket to me while controlling his laugh.

"Okay, now stop laughing.

I actually can stay with you, dadi." I confessed and cuddle in her arms.

"I know beta, we are just teasing you," said, my grandmother.

"Tarini, go and pack your bag now otherwise you will miss your train." said my dad without looking at me.

"What is the train timing?" I asked.

"It's 4:30 P.M. now and your train will come around 7 P.M. which means you have two and a half hours from *now.”*

“Oh.......okay, I think I should start packing now,” I said and left the room.

2 Hours Later

I packed my luggage in around two hours. I only had one bag when I arrived, but I'm leaving with two. I'm taking some of my childhood toys and other belongings, too, and after that, I went straight down to my parents' room. My mom was lying on the bed with two phones in each hand.

"I'm leaving, Maa. Where's papa?" I asked. She stood up and gave me a tight hug.

"Keep my phone with you, and please travel very carefully," Mom recommended.

"No maa, keep your phone, I have already taken your email ID," I unintentionally spill the beans but yes it was true that while packing my bags I snatched her phone for a minute and write her e-mail ID on a piece of paper so that I can talk to Arjuna as princess50 in

Delhi.

"What! Did you say something about email or phone?"
mom enquired.

"Nothing, maa," I said, I'll buy a new phone after
reaching Delhi."

"No! Take mine," Mom insisted.

"Go say bye to grandma, papa and I are waiting at the
main door," she said as she handed over her Phone. I
shook my head and went straight to my grandmother's
room. Her eyes were on the door as she was waiting for
me to come, I entered the room and bow her down for
taking blessing.

"So packed everything?" She asked.

"Yes, Dadi," I answered emotionally.

"So are there any plains for marriage?"

"No Dadi, but why?"

"No..... if you like or love someone then tell me, I will live some more years and see your marriage."

"Dadi! You don't worry, you will live many years from now."

"I had already lived so many years, look I am in my 80s now"

"I know, and you will be living in your 90s and 100s as well, dadi."

"Let's see, It's up to the God," she said.

I shook my head and she continued.

"But you tell me, is there anyone whom you love? Look, don't be shy off of me."

"Umm........there is one dadi but I am however confused, I don't know how to know that the other person is loving or is just pretending." I said.

"Look, Tarini Love is something which you start experiencing naturally, if someone is making an effort to talk to you, if someone is making an effort to meet you every second, that is love and more importantly if *you are also feeling the same way then it is true love."*

"Well, thank you for teaching me the chapters of love dadi, but now I have to go otherwise I will miss my train."

"Yes, go go go.......bye, have a safe journey, and don't forget to call me every day." She said as she puts her hand on my head for blessing me. I slightly emotionally step out of her room and also from the house and arrive at the main door. Papa was in the driving seat of his outmoded Maruti car, which was gifted to him by my grandfather.

After hugging my mom once again, I sat next to my dad, and he started driving the car. 15 minutes passed, and we reach the train station, my train was about to leave. I hugged my dad in a hurry and started running to catch the train. As I boarded up the train, It gives an irritating sound and a jerk and began moving, I waved my hand to my dad from the window until he eloped in the crowd.

He smiled and waved back. I then shifted to my seat and started observing other people. After a while, I went to the upper berth of the train and lay down.

SEVEN

PSYCHO PROPOSE IN BATHROOM

18 Hours Later

As I woke up, I got off my berth. I knot my curly hair and looked towards the window to know about the weather. The sun was hiding behind the gloomy clouds.

"It might rain today." I asserted while unlocking my phone which my mother forcefully gifted me the previous night. The phone's display showed exactly 12:00 A.M. 18 hours had already passed, and I will reach Delhi in more two hours from now and then might meet Arjuna in the evening, I muttered when suddenly his mail arrived.

"Hey good morning princess50"

After reading his e-mail my mind was thinking how he knew that I have just woken up. So I mailed him the same question.

"I don't know, I just woke up an hour ago so I thought I should mail you a morning wish."

"Oo... okay! So you always woke up late or you just did a party last night?"

"Party... it's been ages since I did a party, I was just writing my book last night."

"Why? .....you don't like parties?"

"Umm...Tbh no, I like spending time with my loved ones, and a few close ones" he mailed back after reading his mail.

A little smile appeared on my face perhaps I also like him from the inside,

"I also don't know when was the last time I partied," I said.

"Loved ones! Is tarini on that loved one's list?"

"She's at the top of the list."

Aww...how cute he is, I muttered and suddenly a strong wind started blowing, and all my hair got on my face. I take out my hair band from my bag and tied my curly hair so that no one could see me like Aparichit. Suddenly curiosity about the meeting was all over my mind, and I come up with an idea.

"Okay then I have a piece of promising news for you," I mailed.

"What is that?"

"Do you want to meet Tarini and spend a few minutes with her?"

"Yes just tell me where I have to come, I already have worn my shoes and picked up my car keys." He mailed.

I know it sounds like he's desperately waiting for this.

"Okay then, have you seen the train station near her cafe?"

"Yes!"

"Yep, she is going to be there in an hour."

"Hey, you are not kidding, right?"

"Umm...yes, No! You stupid. Go meet her."

"Okay bye," he mailed back with some bye emoji.

An hour later the train stops with a jerk, I tug my bag and got out of the train station. Many autos were parked in front of the train station. I decided not to take an auto because Arjuna was coming to take me.

"Madam, can I drop you somewhere," said a skinny-looking driver loudly after he came close to me.

"No! My friend is coming," Isaid.

"Arey, madam there's too much traffic, he will not be able to make it here, sit I will drop you." Said the driver as to convince me, his left hand was a little small than the right one, and his eyes were totally on my breast over the conversation. I feel scared, so I took one step back but he too takes a step further.

"Uncle, please go I don't want to travel with you and your auto."

"Since morning I haven't got anything to eat if I drop you somewhere I will get money to eat, please sit inside madam." he now tried to emotionally convince me his last word "Madam" was quite louder and his actions were as If he was trying to grab my hand.

"Look please go otherwise I will call the police." I said firmly and at the same time frightenedly.

"Hey...Tarini! What happened, why you're calling the police?" A voice entered my ears from the left side as I turned my face. I saw Arjuna standing nearly at a distance in his black cargo pants and white hoodie paired with black shoes and transparent glasses. Which were making him look cuter.

As soon as the driver saw him, he sat inside his auto and fled.

"Hey, what are you doing here?" I said pretending like I didn't know he was going to come.

"Umm...I just came to drop off a friend," He lied.

"Oh okay."

"By the way, you're talking about some police or something."

"Nothing forgets that!"

"So tell me how's everything," I asked as if I don't know his feelings nowadays.?

"Umm...Everything is good.

I am writing my new book."

"Oh...okay, so what is it about?"

"About the thing which is now going to happen," He whispered.

"Sorry...I didn't hear that," I said.

"No, it's nothing I will tell you later," he said.

"Secret...huh?" I said.

"No, it's not Secret it's special," he said.

"Ooh...For me," I said my expressions were like I am guessing it, he began laughing I joined him too.

"So you are now going to?"

"Café," I said.

"Come, I will drop you."

"No, I will manage."

"Don't worry, I will charge you a coffee for this." He said with a smile on his face and continued.

"Please come."

"Okay, but where is your car?" I asked.

"Across the road," he said, pointing his hand, but only auto came into my eyes.

"So you came here in an auto?" I asked as I move my face from auto to him.

"No...behind those autos, come I will show you," he clarified and we both traverse the road. A mate brown-colored Audi was parked there behind the autos, Arjuna opened the door with his keys and sat on the driving seat. Till then, I was still outside the car, gazing at the four rings of the Audi.

"Hey, come, I am craving coffee," he said with a smile as if he badly needed that coffee. Smirking, I sat inside the car but not in the first passenger seat but in the backseat of the car just to tease him.

Arjuna looked at me with a prying eye and ignited the car, but he didn't drive the car even an inch until I came and sat on the first seat beside him.

Although he had an Audi, he was driving as slowly as the tortoise runs. Even small kids with mere cycles were coming ahead of us.

"Arjuna, you can speed up the car, the speed limit is 60 here," I suggested.

"Yes, I know, but there is something wrong with the car, sometimes it stops picking the speed and stuck at a very low speed." He lied, and I could sense from his face, he just wanted to spend more and more time with me.

"Your father must be very rich, huh?" I asked.

"Why?"

"No… You are just a new struggling writer, and you have an Audi of your own, It clearly shows that you are from a rich family."

"Mom gifted me this; she works as a CEO in a Pharmaceutical company."

"Woooh… I wasn't expecting this." I said.

"I know, nobody expects this after watching me." He said, and I shook my head with a grin.

"Do you like tea?" I asked him, looking at his face.

Wow, he looks so cute. I whispered.

"Well, it depends with whom I am having the tea," he replied, looking deeply into my eyes.

"You are going to have it with Aslam," I said, and laugh.

"Who Aslam?" He asked curiously.

I pointed towards a small tea shop in the corner of the Gas station, where Arjuna finds out the name on the banner of the shop written "Ashlam Ki Chai."

He halts the car a little ahead of the tea shop.

"Listen, you order Tea, I just come from the washroom," I said.

"Okay!" he symbols me by his head. I get off the car and went directly inside the washroom. He went to the tea shop, ordered the tea, and again sat inside the car.

"Hi @princess50 I am with Tarini" he mailed, and my phone beeped which was on the front seat beside him. He stares at it once, but then he didn't unlock the phone for privacy reasons.

He mailed some more messages and every single time my phone beeped.

After washing my hand, I opened the door of the washroom but abruptly a white cloth got on my whole face and someone again drags me inside the washroom and lock the door from inside.

I screamed, and he tightly clasped and covered my mouth.

"If you didn't stop screaming, you wouldn't be able to laugh again." He said firmly while putting a sharp object on my neck. I nodded my head in fear and try to be quiet as much as I could, His voice sounded as if he was trying to mimic a villain of a 90s Bollywood film. He shifted his hand from my mouth and asked; "Who is @princess50?" In an intense voice.

"I don't know," I said frighteningly. He shoves the sharp object into my neck a little.

"Twinkle, twinkle little star how I wonder if you are telling a lie yes papa I will kill and your body will be mine ha ha ha…" he sings as loudly as many psycho characters used to sing in the movies. He tightly clenches my hair and started dragging me from here to there with my hair. I started sobbing as I got scared and confessed that.

"I am @princess50…"

"Why did you hide your identity?" He asked in a strong voice and thrust me into the corner of the bathroom. My back was fully intact by the wall.

"Uncle, there is a boy named Arjuna, I have liked him since the very first time I saw him but after reading his romantic novel my likeness unconditionally turned into love, and I just to make sure if he also loves that why or not I started talking to him with this account," I said.

"Has he proposed to you yet?"

"No," I said with a soft voice and suddenly the cloth which was on my face went off me and I saw Arjuna standing in front of me while carrying that cloth in his hand. I had understood that now Arjuna knew everything.

"Arjuna… I'm…" I try to say sorry while crying a bit.

"Tarini don't say anything. I love you" he said as he came closer to my lips.

It took me a minute to understand the scenario. I was like is it happening in a real sense, but at that moment I grabbed his neck and gave him a kiss lip to lip. He picks me in his arms amidst kissing. Our bodies felt the warmth of each other and our lips weren't ready to stop biting each other.

After kissing for a few minutes, we both see our life partner in each other's eyes and hugged each other, and then we went inside the car to go to the café. En route, we both didn't talk too much with each other. We were just smirking and watching out from the window, but as we reach the lol café, we both talked endlessly for the very first time. We cuddle and slept together with sparkling eyes and broad smiling faces.

EIGHT

KIDNAPPED BY A LOVER

6 Months Later

After that night, everything changed. Now, most of the time, Arjuna lives here in my café. His book, which nobody was interested in, is now one of the bestselling novels. His bookshelves are now filled full of awards, and he thinks all this is happening only because of me. Sometimes he calls me his lucky charm, good luck. I, too, was enjoying his success and his pure love towards me, but amid all these delightful things, something was bothering me from inside. It was a distressing nightmare that had now become my regular sleeping partner.

"Tarini…tarini……" Arjuna's voice came into my ears and I woke up from my nightmare. My foggy eye was *catching a glimpse of Arjuna and a cup of tea in his hand.*

"Good morning," said Arjuna, and handed over the tea.

"Morning…" I responded in my low, weak voice while taking a sip.

"What happened? That same nightmare again," he raised a question.

"Yeah, I don't know why it's coming again and again," I answered.

"But you never told me what this dream told you."

"Uhh… forgot that Arjuna,

Let's start the day, and you have a flight to catch, right?"

"Yes, but it's in the evening. You tell me what the dream is about." He asked again, this time affectionately while holding my hands.

"Remember I told you about my grandmother a few days back?"

"Yes!"

"Every day she comes into my dreams saying "Marry Arjuna" and then she just fades away. Besides this, I also observe a hospital bed with lots of blood. I don't know why I am seeing all these kinds of things," I described my nightmare.

He started laughing after listening to my nightmares.

"Why are you laughing?" I asked.

"Is it your nightmare or your fetish?" He said sarcastically. I put my cup aside and started tingling him because he gets irritated by it. He, just to get rid of that tingling, grabbed my hand and got closer to my lips. I kissed him, and he joined too, and that's how our morning started with a morning kiss.

Half of the day passes just like that, and now it's time to see the moon. Arjuna had already packed his bags, and now it was time for him to leave. I locked the main door of the café and went inside the car to drop him at the airport and after 15 minutes of the ride, he parked the car on the roadside.

So it's time to go. He held my hand and we both hugged.

"Arjuna, wait… I haven't hugged you properly," I said from a distance.

"And what about the airplane, Tarini?" He sarcastically said with a smile on his face.

"It will wait, too." I let out.

"Why! Is it now your new partner?" He said, lifting me in his arms.

"Yes, at least it could take me to the stars. You are not even taking me to Mumbai."

"Hmm… Yes, you are right, but what if I say that after I come back we can have a nice trip."

"Trip…where?" I asked.

"Ummm…that, I am not going to tell you right now." He smirked and dropped me down on the floor.

"Fuck you!" I said, showing a bit of a tantrum.

"We will do that as well, baby! let me come."

"The bed will be ready for you." I replied, showing my middle finger to become more cool and bitchy.

"And what about you, Tarini?" He asked smirkingly.

I got the car keys from his hand, turned around, and started walking towards the car to avoid him, although I was smiling from the front.

"Hello madam...... I didn't get my answer," Arjuna said, chasing me from my back.

"You will get everything after you come back," I said, and gave him a glance at a smile and closed the car door.

"Uhh...okay, then bye-bye madam girlfriend."

Bye, I said and left. He also traversed the lane and went inside the boarding gate.

A few kilometers passed, and now I was stuck in the middle of the traffic. The road was filled with so many Activa Scooters and Kia cars that, after waiting for some time in the car, I started wondering about the bank balance of these giant vehicle companies. Abruptly, a little girl came to the window holding a few pieces of red roses in her hand. As soon as I noticed her, I slid the car's window to half.

"Didi, these 3 are the last pieces I have left. Please…buy them." The girl requested, pushing the red roses at me.

"Aww… How much for that beta," I asked, emotionally taking a piece of red rose from her hand as I got a little sentimental after observing her.

"Didi, only 30 rupees." the girl said.

"Okay, here you go." I gave her a 100-rupee note to her.

"Didi, I don't have extra money to give you back." the girl said with a priceless smile.

"I don't want the money back, beta. Go have some chocolates with that." I said.

"Thank you! Didi," the girl said with a broad smile and left happily. It's always a joy to put a smile on

someone's face. Joy and happiness are infectious. Spread Love Like Jam and Honey. I smelled the fragrance of the rose and put it on the other seat, then suddenly my eyes became blurry. The dizziness had fully taken over my mind and I started feeling unconscious. Eventually, I fell on the seat.

Many Hours Later

My eyes open, and I observe myself on a hotel bed. Abruptly, I got off the bed and tried to open the door, but it was locked from the outside, so I stopped trying. I went inside the bathroom and started checking myself in the mirror. My face was fully clear. No marks, nothing had happened to me. But the dress which I had put on back then was now fully changed, and now I was in a red gown and red heels, I looked like a diva. Shortly, I heard an unlocking sound on the door and I ran to check. I saw the door open, but no one was there except for a card. I took the card, "come on the helipad right now" was written on it. After reading that card, I got a little scared and thought, I should just run away. I hurriedly started running towards the elevator but as soon as the gate opened I saw a big-fat man with a board in his hand written "please come inside" on it and I did the same as I got terrified by his looks. He pressed the top floor button, and we started going up.

"Listen, I want to go to the reception counter, not to the top floor," I asserted slowly.

He didn't respond and in a few seconds we were on the top of the floor, he pushed me out of the elevator and went back. As I hesitantly walked a few steps ahead just to find out about my surroundings, I came to the centre of the helipad. Then, suddenly, many bulbs and lights started flickering, and the whole area was illuminated in a moment.

An ocean got my attention, which was just in front of me. It was such an amazing sight that I could see the entire thing from there. As I walked a few more steps ahead, I noticed the ocean was filled with many flowers and petals in the written form of "will you marry me, Tarini?". I smiled and started noticing the hot air balloon in the sky, which was filled with my images. I was completely surprised and at the same time so delighted that I forgot everything.

"Will you marry me, Tarini?" a voice entered my ears.

I moved around and saw Arjuna standing there with a ring in his hand.

I got emotional, so I ran toward him and hugged him tightly.

"Will you marry me, Tarini?" He asked again. I stared and slapped him hard.

"Tarini you didn't answer," he said while looking into my eyes.

"Yes, I will marry you. You dumb!" I said emotionally, and he lifted me in his arms up in the air in happiness. Suddenly, the snow machine started pouring snow on us.

We both of us started romping, and he got down on his knees and said:

"Tarini, I love you and if I now know what love is, it is only because of you. I know that it's been only six months to us, but still, I believe that you are my lucky charm. Because of you, I can feel myself slowly, but surely, becoming the me I have always dreamed of being." He put the ring on my ring finger, and we both kissed and enjoyed the night.

NINE

THE SURPRISE ENGAGEMENT

A week ago

"Tring… Tring… Tring," the chime of the doorbell echoed in my ears and I woke up.

The view from the window was still dark. The street lights were blazing in the empty street. I picked up my phone from the side table and checked the time. It was 3:11 A.M. and usually, nobody comes into the café at this point, although Arjuna sometimes came late from his book signing events and meetings, but today it was unusual as he was with me sleeping next to me on the bed.

"Arjuna…arjuna….arjuna" I tried to wake him up.

"Yes, you are looking gorgeous, baby." He said in a dozing voice, without even taking his head out of the blanket.

"Arjuna woke up and saw someone ringing the bell at the main door," I said.

"Then please go and open the door. Someone must be waiting."

"Arrey, but who can come at this point in time? Arjuna, It's only 3:11 AM," I said, and he quickly responded by jumping out of his blanket.

"What…who is at the main door right now then?" He questioned.

"Do I have any kind of special powers?"

"No!" He promptly answered.

"Then how would I know?" I annoyingly said.

"Okay fine! Come, let's find out who is at the gate." He said and unlocked our room's door. We both went towards the main entrance, crossing through the reception area. The bell was still chiming.

"Hey, wait," I whispered.

"But why, and why are you whispering?" He reacted.

"Arjuna, I think we should take something with us for our self-defense and protection. He could be a thief as well," I whispered.

"Don't worry, I am with you. Nothing will happen, let's go now." He tried to become the hero of the moment.

"Hulk too needs a hammer, baby! Please go and grab something." I advise him.

"Okay, wait!" He went inside and arrived in a second with a party popper in his hand.

"Okay, now open the door." He asserted.

"What opened the door? What will you do with the party popper? Celebrate the thief's birthday." I said.

"Yes, just open the damn gate now, It's been continuously ringing."

As I opened the main entrance, I glimpsed a man standing with two women carrying bouquets in their hands, which were completely covering their faces. I got confused while, at the same time, was curious to know about the visitor, suddenly Arjuna popped the popper, and they all revealed their faces by removing the bouquets from their faces.

It was Arjuna's mom and my parents. Looking at them, my curiosity had now been changed into shockingness. I was in awe and didn't believe their appearances, but then both the mothers came forward and hugged me, handing the bouquets to make me believe that I was not dreaming. I pass on the bouquets to Arjuna just the same way ministers pass their bouquets to their PA's or managers.

"Come! Maa, Papa, Aunty. Please come inside!"

"Obviously, we will come," said my dad jovially, and they all went into the café and then to our living room. Both mothers put their feet up on the couch and occupied the whole couch. While Arjuna offers a chair to my father, I and he grab one.

"Auntie, Maa, you guys need tea?" Arjuna asked.

Both the mothers said yes by nodding.

"Without sugar, beta," my dad gave instructions.

"Yes, uncle," Arjuna said, standing up from the chair and went to the kitchen. I was still in shock, looking at them.

"Beta, what happened, why are you looking so surprised?" Arjuna's mom asked.

"No, Aunty!, I am just confused about all this. I mean, when did you guys plan this surprise visit," I asked.

We...Arjuna's mom started to explain, but my mom was herself and cut Arjuna's mom in the middle.

"None of us had planned this surprise visit, Tarini." My mom asserted cutting Arjuna's mom.

"Then who did?" I inquired.

"Well, ask your future husband." My mom said trying to be the coolest in the room.

They all shake their belly with laughter.

"Future husband...who?" I questioned.

"The one who is making tea for us in the kitchen" answered my dad.

"I think you guys need water," I said and left the living room.

"She gets shy, I think." I gave attention to my dad's voice from the back.

"Arjuna, did you plan all this?" I asked as I entered the kitchen.

"Yes, and you can later give me a kiss for this act of kindness, baby." He said, adjusting his hair with confidence.

"Why later? I can kiss you right now. Come on! Give me your cheeks." I said, getting closer to him.

"Tarini, our parents are here!" He said and tried to let me realize.

"So what?" I said.

Then he brought his cheek forward, and I slapped him so hard on the cheek that its sound went into the living room.

"What happened? What type of sound was this?" The parents asked together from the living room.

"Nothing… Arjuna dropped a vessel in excitement," I lied from the kitchen.

"Why did you slap me?" He asked after the slap.

It took him a few seconds to infer what had happened.

"Then what, I should kiss you?" I said in a bit of anger.

"That's what you were supposed to do, right?"

"Arjuna, tell me why the parents are here and what's cooking in your mind," I asked.

"Well, that's another surprise for you." He said with a smile.

"Well, do you need another slap?" I said, flaunting my wrist.

"No, no... I don't need anything right now, but our parents need the tea." He said turning off the gas and started staining the tea.

"Arjuna, tell me what is going on in your mind," I asked him sweetly this time.

"You know what! A writer never reveals his story before it has been launched," he whispered in my ears and went to the living room with five cups of tea on a tray. I, too, followed him.

"Uncle, your tea without sugar." He served my dad, then both the mothers and then me. He grabs one cup and sits next to me and then everyone enjoyed the old stories of my father which he began conversing as he started sipping the tea. After some minutes, my father finished the story and everyone finished the tea too.

"I guess you guys must be tired out, right?" I asked.

"Yes, very much!" said Arjuna's mom.

"Yes, I also think you guys should take some rest now," said Arjuna.

"Oh yes, I also want a good nap," said, my dad.

Arjuna then took my parents to the other room so that they can sleep effortlessly.

I share my bed with Arjuna's mom in my bedroom, and he nodded off on the living room couch.

5 Hours Later

The sun had now fully risen and the clock on the wall was showing 10:20 A.M.

I woke up and noticed that Arjuna's mom was not on the bed. I went inside the bathroom, but as I entered I saw that the mirror was covered with a red transparent saree. I removed it, "Hi love, remember last night I told you about another surprise. Be ready in this red saree ASAP because your surprise is getting cold" was written on the mirror with red lipstick. He also had scribbled a heart on the lowest of the mirror.

I smiled with love and carried the saree to wear it. I was enjoying the moment and was happy to know the fact that my future husband is so, so, so... romantic.

After taking the bath, I started to blow dry my hair when Arjuna's voice message beeped on the phone screen.

"Hi love, look how pretty you are looking in this red saree today,

I think the mirror will get shy after seeing you like this but still, something is missing", I gave my ears to his voice message. After listening to his voice message, the first thing I did was I tried to find him in my room, but disappointedly I couldn't find him in the room because he wasn't there. "How without being here he knew that I am looking pretty in this red saree?" I whispered.

A volume of drone entered the room through the window. Many red-hearted shape balloons were tied to it with a box. As the drone came closer, I grabbed the box and the drone fly back. I opened the box, there was a small note on the top.

"Hey Miss Pretty, you must be thinking how I knew you looked pretty in that red saree, so let me tell you it was not the saree that made you look pretty, you look pretty in everything. But this box has something for you," was written on the note.

There were 3 other small boxes in the box. I took them all out and opened them one by one, in one of the boxes were red high heels, in the other red bangles, and in a small but nicely designed box was a red bindi. I put them all on and ended up in front of the mirror and was amazed to see myself, not because of beauty or anything, but because I had described the same outfit to my mother in my childhood as my wedding outfit. After all that, it was clear to me that Arjuna was up to something bigger this time.

Suddenly, his voice message beeped once again.

"Hey, come to the café area."

I quickly took a look in the mirror and made my way to the café area. The floor of the café was filled with red roses and red heart-shaped balloons. The walls were completely decorated with my pictures and pink and white roses. There was also a black stage in the middle of the café, but no one was there. I stepped on the red roses and headed straight for the stage. Unexpectedly, the lights went out.

"I know it's not our birthday, but it's still a special day for us. Tarini, I met you when things weren't going well in my life and no one wanted to read my book. Do you remember the first day I came to your café to introduce my book? I failed miserably that day, but I was glad because I met you. When I went to bed that day, I couldn't sleep well because I kept thinking about your face all night. Your smile had taken my soul forever and ever, I love you. Will you please marry me?" Came his voice from all directions, and suddenly he came from behind, when I turned around I saw him on his knees in a red kurta and gold pyjamas with a box with a diamond ring.

"Will you marry me, Tarini?" He asked as he took the diamond ring out of the box.

I began to blush, my face had now turned pink, and my wide smile made no effort to stop smiling. I looked at him with love for him in my eyes.

"Will you marry me, Tarini?" He asked again.

"Forever and ever I'll marry you," I confess and kiss him on the lips, then the red roses start raining on us along with red heart-shaped balloons.

Suddenly I hear some people cheering and clapping as I see our parents at the entrance of the café and a crowd of at least 50 people behind them. Some of them *were my cousins, friends, and relatives while some of them were Arjuna's school friends and his relatives who all set foot inside the café.*

They all looked alluring as they were all dressed in ethnic robes. I stared at Arjuna and hugged him, while my inner self said how happy I was. Everything felt like a fairy tale. Both mothers came to me, hugged me, and took me to the door where I looked at a banner that said "Welcome to Arjuna and Tarini's ring ceremony" after looking at it, I looked at my mother and then Arjuna's mother and hugged them both tightly.

That day felt like it was my own fictional world. I walked back to the black stage, Arjuna and I were ready to put the ring on each other's fingers. I looked at my mom, she was standing holding the video call from Dadi while dadi blessed us over the video call. Arjuna put the ring on my finger, and my father also took out a diamond ring from his pocket and gave it to me. I knelt and put the diamond ring on Arjuna's finger.

Everyone started clapping and cheering again, and some of Arjuna's classmates shouted, "Kiss her…kiss her, brother…kiss…kiss…" Arjuna looked at me and kissed me on the cheek, which made me feel a little shy in front of everyone, even though I was floating on air from inside. Besides, everyone gathered and formed a circle, someone played a romantic song and asked us to dance as a couple. We had danced as a couple an infinite number of times, but that day the feeling was different. Feelings that never exist otherwise, a sense of love, caring, and happiness was in the air. After the couple's dance, we all drank beer, ate, cut the cake and then the loud music started to play and everyone started to dance. With every dance movement, the day also passed and now all the cousins, relatives, and friends congratulated us and went back to their joy of life.

Both our parents got tired after the celebration and decided to have a nap. After all the guests had gone back, I closed the front door and sat down on the black stage in the middle of the café, thinking about how I had imagined it all when I was a child. And now it was taking place in just a few hours, but those few hours were truly tremendous.

"Here is coffee for you." Arjuna came with a cup of coffee and sat down next to me on the black stage.

"Thank you," I said as I took the cup from him and held his hand.

"Why don't you drink coffee?" I asked.

"Nothing, just my tongue got a few ulcers"

"What?" Show me.

"Do not worry, it's nothing"

"Arjuna show it to me!" I insisted, and he showed me his tongue.

"Does it hurt?" I asked.

"Forget it, tell me, do you like the surprise?" He asked.

"I totally liked it, you know what, if you had asked me today if we were going to get married, I would have agreed too," I said.

"Oh, that means I am missing a great opportunity today," he said with a smile.

"No, you did not miss anything, I will marry you whenever you want." I said, putting my head on his shoulder, and continued; "You know, Arjuna, I have always wished to have someone like you in my life who cares for me, respects me, and more importantly, loves me and adores me so much, I promise you that I will never leave you, not even for a second," I get a little sentimental.

"I know you will never leave me, Tarini." He said, and neither of us knew when we fell asleep.

TEN

LYING BODY BLOOD

4 Hours Later

"Arjuna....Tarani....arjuna wake up children," my father's voice reached our ears and we both woke up while rubbing our blurry eyes.

"Good morning, uncle," said Arjuna without opening his eyes properly.

"Beta, the night has just begun, it is only 9 PM," my father said and smiled. Arjuna opened his eyes properly and looked around.

"Oh yes, it's still night, sorry uncle, I thought..."

"Now practice calling me dad, and do not call me uncle Arjuna."

"Okay, uncle. Oh, sorry, papa."

They were both laughing when I open my eyes. I see my father standing in front of us in a red kurta and white pyjamas. Suddenly, both mothers enter the café area wearing a red and white Bengali saree that matched their dresses.

"Where you all are going?" I asked.

"Shri Laxmi Narayan Temple," replied my mother.

"Uncle.....sorry, dad, mom, you can also go there tomorrow morning," Arjuna suggested.

"No, Beta, now is the best time as there will be fewer gatherings in the temple," Arjuna's mother explained.

"Okay! Then take my car, I'll just bring you the keys," Arjuna said and took a step towards the bedroom.

"We will take the cab, beta, do not worry," my father said.

"No dad, look at the dark clouds, it might rain and besides the car is just parked." Arjuna insisted and offered my father the car keys, he accepted, and we all went to the parking lot. The mothers got in the back seat of the car and of course, my father got in the driver's seat, and they drove off.

Arjuna closed the door and we both went back to the café area.

"Arjuna I am starving, do you need Maggie? I will cook it," I asked.

"Yes, please! But I just came from the washroom."

"Okay, come quickly," I said, and he went into the bathroom. I took the knife and started cutting the vegetables, and suddenly it started raining, and the clouds started rumbling. I wanted to close the window, but when the lightning of the thunderstorm hit my face, I took a step back and set about preparing Maggie.

12 minutes later

"Arjuna, come quickly or your hot soup Maggie will turn into cold Coca-Cola," I said as I placed the bowl of Maggie on the living room sofa and sat down with it.

Another 10 minutes passed, and he was still in the bathroom.

"Arjuna, what are you cooking? It took me 10 minutes to cook the 2-minute Maggie, and you can not manage to cook it in 20 minutes." I made fun of him, but he did not respond. It was pouring rain and the wind was destroying many plants and street lights. I went to the bathroom to check, but when I knocked on the door, it was opened, and I saw Arjuna lying on the red, bloody floor. I did not understand what had happened, I just stood there looking at Arjuna and the blood he had vomited.

A second later, I came back to my senses and tried to wake him up by sprinkling water on him, but he did not respond. I got scared, ran into the living room, and called our parents. I tried to call them several times, but none of their phones responded. Sometimes it said, "The number you are trying to reach is not in service," and sometimes it said, "The number you are trying to reach is either not in service or talking to someone else." I went back into the bathroom and lifted him into my arms. Because of the heavy rain, the streets were deserted. By now, my red saree had turned a deep red from his blood. I ran along the middle of the street with him in my arms. With every step I took, the situation got worse and worse, I fell over countless times on the street because his weight completely soaked us both.

Suddenly came a black and yellow colored car.

"Hello, madam! Get in quickly," said the driver as he got up from his driver's seat and helped me put Arjuna in the back seat, and when we were all seated, he began the drive. The roads were flooded with water, so the car was going extremely slow, but somehow we reached the nearby hospital. A couple of hospital workers came with the stretcher and placed Arjuna on it. In a minute Arjuna was taken to the ICU, and I was waiting outside the ICU where several doctors were coming in and out every minute.

"Doctor, what happened to him, how is he now?" I asked a doctor who came out of the ICU room.

"Ma'am, we are doing our best, please calm down."

"How can I be calm when my beloved is in pain," I screamed at him and started crying. The doctor instructed the nurse to take care of me and left. An old nurse stood in front of me, I looked at her, and she held my hand and looked into my eyes, I hugged her as if she were my mother and began to cry. At first, she did not react, but then she rubbed her hand on my head and I slept on the floor.

8 Hours Later

I opened my eyes and was lying on the floor. I got up and looked into the ICU room. Suddenly, the door opened, and the doctor came out.

"Doctor, how is he now?" I asked.

"We are trying, I can not say anything at the moment, but please do not worry, we will try our best, and please inform your parents," said the doctor and left.

I went to the pharmacy and asked for his phone and called my father.

"Hello," my father answered.

"Dad," my slow, nervous voice.

"Hello...hello,"

"Tarini, where are you, Beta, and where is Arjuna?" He inquired.

"Dad, come to the hospital, I'll send you a text message with the location," I said and interrupted the call and sent the location via text message. After half an hour both mothers came along with my father when I saw them I ran to them and hugged them all and explained what had happened. Arjuna's mother burst into tears, but somehow my mother managed to help her. My parents were also shocked.

"Are you relatives of Arjuna Bhatt?" A nurse asked.

Yes!, my father replied.

"The doctor is calling you to his cabin," said the nurse, and we all went to his cabin.

"Sir, what happened to him? Is he all right now?" I asked.

"Ma'am, I am sorry, but he has stage 3 blood cancer and his condition is really bad, but we are trying our best," the doctor explained.

We were all shocked and could not believe what the doctor had just said.

"Doctor, when will he be well again?" Arjuna's mother asked with hope.

"Ma'am can not say anything yet, have patience, said the doctor and left his cabin."

2 Days Later

It has been two days now, and I have not moved an inch from the ICU. Both mothers went with my father for a tea break, and I was outside the ICU room.

"Beta, have this," my father said as he brought me the tea and some cookies.

"No, Dad, I do not want anything," I said.

"Eat something, Beta," you have not eaten for two days, my father said, but I did not answer. Suddenly, the door of the intensive care unit opened, and a doctor hurriedly came out to us.

"What happened, doctor?" I asked as he came closer.

"Are you Tarini?" He asked immediately.

"Yes, doctor, but what happened, is he all right?"

"He regained consciousness a few hours ago, and since then he has been taking only your name.

Please come with me" said the doctor.

"Beta, you go, I just came informing the mothers," my father said.

I gave him a sign of okay and went into the ICU room following the doctor.

Arjuna was lying on the bed, and several doctors were around him. I ran to him and took his hand, he looked at me and began to cry without having a voice. I also started crying looking at him like that.

The doctors also became emotional and left us alone for a few moments.

"Uhh, Ooo, ree…" *Arjuna tried to speak, but because of the ulcers, he was unable to.*

"Okay, don't worry, do not worry. I am listening to you" *I said and kissed his hand with love.*

"Ooo uhh reee," *he tried to speak again, but unexpectedly he vomited blood.*

"Arjuna………what happened?" *I panicked, but he did not let go of my hand and signalled me to get him a piece of paper that was lying there on a small table. I grabbed the paper and handed it to him. He looked for a pen, but could not find it anywhere, so he put his ring finger in his mouth, which was all red and filled with blood. As he put his ring finger in his mouth, he spits blood again, and I got scared.*

"Arjuna, please let me call the doctors," *I said, but he did not let go of my hand and even held it tighter. He put his finger in his mouth again, which was now smeared with more and more blood, and wrote something on the white paper with his blood and handed it to me. He used his finger as a pen.*

Suddenly, the ICU door opened, and the doctors came in and ran toward us. Two doctors grabbed my hand and pulled me out of the ICU, but Arjuna wasn't letting me go He was not leaving my hand while in the moment of scrimmage I looked into Arjuna's emotional eyes, he was crying from his heart, and his eyes were saying that he didn't want me to leave him, but the doctors pulled me out of the ICU and closed the door. By then I had completely lost control of myself and started screaming, crying and hitting the wall, and kicking the chairs here and there, but suddenly Arjuna's mother appeared in front of me and wiped my tears.

"How is he, what happened to him?" Arjuna's mother asked faithfully.

"Nothing, auntie, I just met him. He is fine," I lied straightforwardly. She hugged me with emotion and began to cry while thanking God with her hand, and we all hugged together.

"Tarini beta, can I see him for a moment?" Arjuna's mother asked.

"No, auntie, not now, he is resting," I said because I know she can not see him like this.

"Okay... but next time I will meet him. You know, he called me every day, and now I have not talked to him

for two days."

"Okay auntie, only you will meet him next time," I assured her and took a step toward the elevator

"Where are you going, beta," my mother asked from behind.

"Washroom!" I said and went to read the letter Arjuna had given me in the ICU.

When I entered the elevator, there were many people inside, so I dropped the idea of reading the letter in the elevator and went to the washroom, which was vacant, I closed the door and started reading.

"Please complete my last book Tarini, I want you to finish it for me and launch it in our café. I would not say promise me because I know you will do it for me, I love you forever," he had written in the letter.

After reading the letter, I became emotional, my eyes could not stop crying, but after a point, I got myself under control and promised to complete his unfinished book and went back to our parents outside the ICU.

"Dad, you take care of everything, I am going back to the café," I said as I walked to them.

"But what happened?" Arjuna's mother asked.

"I just made him a promise, auntie, and I will not go back to him until I fulfil the promise I made to him," I said with a fiery confidence burning in my heart.

"Do you really mean it now, Tarini," my mother said.

"Yes! Maa, before he gets well and takes me in his arms, I will have fulfilled the promise I made to him," I said, and left.

ELEVEN

THE LAST PROMISE

Finally, after an hour, I reached the café, but as I entered the café, all the things that had happened that night came to my mind. I fell down on the sofa and stared at the stuffed Maggie bowl I had cooked for Arjuna that night. I stared at it for many minutes and the memories of the last 3 days came into my psyche, again and again, Arjuna's screaming and crying voices entering my ears. Furthermore, I took the Maggie bowl and threw it against the wall and broke it into hundreds of pieces in anger, but still, Arjuna's screaming voice and face came to my mind, it did not stop at all. I splashed water on my face and started screaming, dancing here and there, but still, his voice and face kept appearing in my mind, and suddenly I fell on the floor.

1 Day Later

"Ring….ring….ring," I heard from the entrance of the café and woke up from the floor. The shards of the broken Maggie bowl were still on the floor. I ignored it and went straight to the entrance and opened the gate.

"Hi, (after a second) do you remember me," a girl said.

"No!" I said, trying to remember.

Dhara "The delivery girl! Do you remember, I dropped you off at the train station?"

"OOO, yes," I remember.

"What do you want?"

"I quit my old job, and now I am looking for a new one." She said.

"Do you know how to make coffee?" I asked.

"I know it very well," she answered quickly.

"Okay, then come from tomorrow, here is the key." I handed her the key to the café.

Thank you, "but what is my job here? Am I the receptionist or the waitress?"

"You will control the whole café, make coffee for the guests and serve them, and yes, never ask me any questions, or you will be out of a job immediately."

"Okay.......see you tomorrow." She said and left. I closed the door and started cleaning the whole café area, one by one. I never wanted any staff in my cafe but now the circumstances are different I can not handle my cafe at this tough phase of my life and also I need to consolidate in writing arjuna's book.

After almost an hour, I logged into Arjuna's laptop. He was working on a project called "My Last Wish" I pressed enter and opened the file. There was only the last chapter left to write, but he had already written down the name of the last chapter, which was "My First Love" I tried to write something, but I failed immediately. I tried to write many things several times, but each time I postponed them again. Suddenly, my phone rang.

"Hello Beta," my father's voice.

"Yes, dad," I answered.

"*Beta, we just met Arjuna in the ICU, he is recovering.*"

"*I know dad. He will get better soon,*" *I said.*

"*When we entered the ICU, beta, he was looking for you. I suggest you come and see him.*"

"*No, Dad, I made him a promise, and I will not meet him until his unfinished book is finished*"

"*But Beta,*" *he tried to say, but I interrupted him and said,* "*Papa, I know he'll wait for me,*" *I said and ended the call to get back into writing the story.*

2 Weeks Later

Fourteen days have passed, and I have neither met him nor spoken to him. My soul was now impatiently waiting to embrace him, but I still could not meet him.

In the last 2 weeks, I have finished editing his book and had a meeting with his book publisher, and now I am on my way to pick up the first copies of his book from the printer and then launched it in our café.

As I entered the printing publication house, I saw a plethora of books and magazines stored in a bundle, but my eyes stopped when I saw the copies of Arjuna's book. There were more than 100 copies of his book.

"Hello, ma'am," the publication manager greeted me.

"Hello, I am looking for my......"

"I know, ma'am. Here are the first copies of Arjuna's sir books," he said, stopping me in the middle and handed over a box full of Arjuna's books.

"Thank you!" I said and turned to leave, but he stepped in from behind.

"Ma'am, can you please do me a favor, My daughter is a big fan of Arjuna sir, she loved his first book. Could you please tell him?" the manager asked.

"Yes, I will tell him and thank your daughter for reading it," I said and took a step to leave, but suddenly turned around and called the manager from behind.

He turned around and took a few steps toward me.

"Sir, please give the first copy to your daughter," I said and offer a copy out to him.

"Thank you so much, ma'am. She will love it," said the manager with a happy expression on his face. I smiled and walked away.

After a while I came back to the café, when I opened the front gate I saw that the café was filled with so many people, every single seat was occupied. I went to the center of the café, pulled out a chair, and built a pyramid with Arjuna's latest book. Only a few people stared at me, while some were busy with their work.

When I stopped building the pyramid, I went to each chair and asked them to move their chairs and face me. Some people did, others did not, but I pushed my way to the center of the café and began to read the first chapter of his book.

"Please read the second chapter!" many people insisted.

"The book is here and everyone can take it, but now I have to go"

I said and left the café with a copy of his book in my hand. I very happily rushed in a car to the hospital. I took the elevator and went to the ICU floor. An ambiguous emptiness was there on that day, don't know why, but ignoring that, I excitedly entered the ICU room. I saw Arjuna in the hospital bed staring at the ceiling while smiling. Furthermore, I walked up behind him and slept on his small hospital bed next to him and hugged him tightly.

"You know I love you, I love you, I love you, everyone in the café loves your book, and today I met a little fan of yours too. Actually, I met her father. You know writing is so hard, Arjuna, it took me 14 days to finish just one chapter.

"Think if I had decided to become a writer how many years it would take me to write my first book," I said with a smile and a heart full of affection, but he did not answer.

"Arjuna, why don't you say something, say something na."

"Arjuna..." I insisted, but he did not respond.

"Arjuna, if you do not answer me this time, I will slap you," I said.

He still did not respond, and I slapped him, but he did not respond. I slapped him again and he did the same. The room was completely silent, and I could hear the wall clock "Tick-Tick" with each passing second. I hear the sound of footsteps at my back. I turned around and saw my father slowly walking towards me, cleaning his eyes.

"Dad, what happened?" I inquired after noticing tears in his eyes and dissatisfaction on his face. He looked me in the eyes, hugged me, and started crying loudly. I was still confused and did not know what had happened, Why was he crying, Why wasn't Arjuna answering? All these thoughts hit my mind with a heavy hammer as my father murmured in a low sobbing voice.

"Beta Arjuna is no more, we have lost him, you have lost him forever."

"Dad please, (I pause) You know I do not like this kind of joke, especially about Arjuna. I know and God knows we are made to live forever," I said confidently, and took a step back. My father finally burst out louder from the emotions he had been in control of since he got off my back.

"Arjuna, if I find this is a prank, I am going to kill you," I asserted while looking at Arjuna, but he still was not ready to answer. My father's tears were not stopping, then Arjuna's mother entered the room along with my mother. Both were emotional and crying, his mother was uncontrollable, throwing her legs here and there, hitting the walls, and acting like she had gone crazy. Besides the mother, there were 3 nurses trying to

control her. All this crying sadness and uncontrollable grief of his mother scared me and made me panic. I didn't dare to take that much, so I grabbed the bottle of Saline from the shelf next to Arjuna's bed, opened it, and splashed it in his face, but he was still the same obtuseness.

The crying sound coming from my back, the sadness on my father's face, and the unanswered Arjuna on the bed made me shudder inside. I wasn't ready to cry because my soul wasn't yet ready to accept the fact that he'd left me at the very beginning of our journey, but the tears from my eyes sank to the floor. Since my childhood, I've often cried, but today, at that moment, it was something different, I cried from the bottom of my heart, without making a sound, without showing any reaction, I just looked at his mortal body.

"Arjuna woke up…" I cried out loudly and started hitting him, throwing everything I had in my hand at him, and hugging and kissing him at the same time. The nurses looked at me sympathetically at first and tried to understand my feelings for Arjuna, but then they started to take me out of the ICU when they realized that I was hitting Arjuna hard and the situation became uncontrollable.

"I'm sorry, but please stop this and come with us," one of the nurses said as she grabbed my shoulders from behind. I don't know why, but her authoritarian voice didn't feel good to me, so out of anger I gave her a resounding slap and continued to throw objects at

Arjuna. Immediately, the other nurses pounced on me angrily, pulling my hair and throwing me to the floor. My father sprinted toward me, but the nurses kept him at a distance, and they both pulled me out of the ICU and threw me on the floor like a pile of garbage. I got up and ran to the ICU door, but the nurse beat me to it and locked the door from the inside. I started banging on the door, throwing flower pots and chairs at the door, but it didn't break. I get unconscious and, sat on the floor with the support of the wall, getting emotionless.

The doctor came to me a minute later and held my hand.

"I'm sorry Tarini, he was really a good person. I treated him like my own son. He used to tell me how he proposed to you on the helipad and how the two of you started chatting using your mother's email address, he told me everything and just before he died he asked me to tell you something, he said: It wasn't your fault or his fault, it was just the destiny of this relationship."

The doctor tapped me on my shoulder and left emotionally.

And that's how our story ended!

9 798888 838747